SPITE AND PRIDE

VALERIE PURI

First Edition. Printed in the United States of America.

ISBN-13: 978-1-7324825-1-7

Editing Services Provided by Juli's Elite Editing

Cover Created by Phycel Designs

Interior Formatting by Dark Crown Press

Chapter One

Spite and pride motivated me to exact my revenge. For years I endured the unrelenting insults and belittling of my rival, Emery Bernand. Upon our first business meeting, many years ago, he greeted me with the words, "Alex, you've got a big personality for a short man." He laughed as he clapped a merry hand against my back. Offended, I bared my teeth in a forced smile.

The most egregious insult, however, was when Emery and my fiancé, Justine, had an affair. I was furious when I found out. I destroyed my apartment in a fit of rage. I broke priceless plates, slashed valuable paintings, and cast pictures of my fiancé into the fire. As I sat and contemplated my misplaced destruction, I realized my actual target was Emery.

When I heard news that he had fallen into financial trouble, I seized the opportunity to rub it in his face. His finances could no longer keep up with his extravagant lifestyle, and bankruptcy was imminent. I, most generously mind you, offered to purchase his ancestral home and rid him of the financial burden of the sprawling estate.

During the property closing, Emery could barely meet my eyes as the notary presented him with a pen. He fumbled with shaky hands as he initialed the document. My grin broadened when his hand slipped and dropped the pen while signing on the last line. It was done. The home that had been in his family for generations was mine. I gripped the keys to the estate triumphantly as I watched him walk slowly from the room, his head hung low.

The locals called the estate Bernand Manor - a name I detested. The first thing I did when I took possession of my rival's former home, was remove the monogrammed gates at the end of the drive.

Even my fiancé begged me to take her back after Emery's financial ruin. She wanted to live a life of wealth and comfort. That, Emery could no longer give. But I could. I renewed our engagement on the condition she would never be alone with Emery again.

While strolling through my new home, I inhaled the sweet scent of victory. It smelled like freshly polished mahogany. I quite enjoyed exploring my new mansion. I took possession of the home and everything inside - his furniture, books, draperies, appliances, and even his collection of fine suits. Perhaps I would have them tailored to fit me. Emery was a fat man, but he had excellent taste.

As I explored, I discovered secret tunnels and chambers. There were many concealed entrances to passageways connecting rooms and wings of the estate.

I learned of an area of particular interest to me: a hidden chamber directly beneath the ballroom. I stumbled upon it, while running my hand along the wall of the hallway as I walked. My fingers detected a slight ridge in the wood paneling, stopping me in my tracks. I inspected the surface, running my hand up and down the ridge until I felt the tiniest of latches - more of a button to be exact - hidden within the wood.

Pressing the button, the panel swung inward, revealing a curved staircase descending into the darkness. I took out my flashlight, which I always carried on me while exploring the estate. I clicked it on and illuminated the path before me.

Cold welcomed me as I descended into the forgotten depths. A thick layer of dust carpeted the flagstone floor. No one had tread across these stones for many decades. I may have been the first to explore this chamber in near a hundred years.

The space was gloomy, yet inviting with wide pillars holding up the vaulted brick ceiling. After exploring every crevice within the spacious room, I discovered there was one way in, and one way out. At the far end of the room, I found a niche with rubble nearby. The loose stones seemed out of place in the otherwise intact chamber. I would have to fix it, but in my own way.

The secret chamber inspired the most delectable revenge fantasy - one I thought to play out in reality. And so, I arranged a party. Not just any party, but a masquerade ball. The invitations went out in the post, calling all elite members of society to my newly acquired home. I hand delivered the card to my enemy; I wanted to see the look on Emery's face when he received an invitation to his ancestral home. It was an insult to his pride that I had to experience firsthand.

"Emery," I said, "I want to personally invite you to my home for a masquerade ball. All the important members of society will be there, so you must come."

With such an invitation, he was compelled to attend. I grinned with malicious delight when he accepted. The first part of my plan was set in motion.

"Excellent. I will see you in two weeks. I believe

you already know the location, so you don't need directions," I jeered.

The jab worked. His face twisted in an expression of hurt pride, yet he fought to maintain his composure.

Two weeks felt like two years. I wanted to execute my plan immediately, but the delay gave me time to prepare. I gathered all the materials needed and placed them strategically in the secret chamber beneath the ballroom.

Chapter Two

At long last, the evening of my reckoning arrived. Every light in the three-story mansion was lit, the impression grand as my guests drove up my private road. The century-old trees lining the path only added to the majesty of my new estate.

Here I was, a self-made man of new wealth who purchased the ancestral home of my enemy: Emery Bernand. He was now a ruined man of old wealth. For all the advantages and money handed to him, it couldn't save him from the poorhouse. I chuckled at the thought.

I opened the door to welcome Emery to my new home, my fiancé - the same woman he had an affair with - on my arm. I wanted to rub the fact that Justine was mine in his face. He had her for a brief period, but couldn't keep her. She was mine and always would be.

Justine looked like embodied wealth: her neck sparkled with a million dollars' worth of diamonds. The red dress clinging seductively to her body set me back a few grand on top of it. Her red fox mask hadn't cost much. The rubies I added to it, however, did. The money was trivial. All I cared about was making her look as though he could never afford her.

"Emery, my old friend," I said as I embraced him. "Welcome. I'm so pleased you could come. I can't wait to show you some improvements I've made to the place." I waved my hand dismissively. "But there will be time for that. For now, let's enjoy ourselves and mingle with my guests. You remember Justine, right?"

She pursed her crimson lips in disgust, no doubt uncomfortable staring at her ex-lover. The man who had probably promised her the world was now penniless. I didn't mind rubbing it in her face either. Let it be a lesson to her: no man could take care of her as I could, so she better not think about cheating on me again.

Emery said nothing but offered a wary smile.

I pointed to my jester mask. "I see you forgot this was a masquerade."

Emery looked around at my guests, all dressed the part.

"I must have run out of time to buy a mask," he said.

Run out of time or money?

"Don't worry, I have a selection of spares you can choose from. Oliver! Bring that tray over here to our guest."

My butler approached carrying a large silver platter containing a variety of masks. Each one was a unique animal: a sheep, crow, bat, lion, deer, and a wolf.

Emery chose the wolf mask and put it on. Pity, I pictured him as more of a sheep.

I excused myself from his company and mingled with the rest of my guests. They marveled at the magnificence of my masquerade ball. As well as music and dancing, contortionists and ribbon dancers dawning harlequin masks provided entertainment throughout the night.

The evening wore on and my wine cache nearly ran dry. It was all worth it, though. My guests were fed, drunk, and happy. And I had the perfect stage for my revenge.

This would be the last night anyone would see Emery alive. Every guest here could provide me with an alibi. They could attest to the quality time I spent with each one of them. I wouldn't have had time to cause any harm to my treasured friend, Emery.

I, and each of my guests, could only assume that the pressure of the evening was too much for him. Coming to a party in the home that had been in his family for generations - the home he lost because of his squandered fortune - must have overwhelmed him.

Perhaps he took his own life. Perhaps he left the city altogether to start a new life, free of the social ties and high expectations of his past. Either way, I couldn't be accused of having any involvement in his disappearance. My story was sound. My alibi secured. My plan was perfect.

Chapter Three

As I tread across the parquet floor of the ballroom, what I saw in the far corner enraged me. That minx Justine and Emery were flirting. I could tell by the way she held her drink, holding it so the rim of the glass just touched her lower lip. She cocked her hip out to the side so the slit in her dress exposed her long leg.

Emery was standing too close to her. I watched his mouth move as he spoke, but I was too far away to hear the words. I saw them both raise their glasses and toast each other. Justine licked her lips slowly after she took a sip of her wine.

I had seen enough. The time had come for me to execute my plan for Emery. I would deal with Justine later.

I barged in on their scene with false merriment.

"Emery, come! I must show you the most extraordinary thing."

I grabbed him by the arm and led him away, leaving the ballroom, the crowd, and Justine behind.

"After moving in, I explored this sprawling estate, taking in all its majesty. Some areas needed major renovations, like the master suite - that entire area was a design disaster. The orange color I had painted on the walls is quite an improvement," I said.

I never put gaudy orange paint on the walls, nor did I renovate that room. It was actually tasteful how Emery kept it. I just didn't want to tell him that. I knew he prized his private suite in his castle and I wanted to rattle him, make him think I destroyed something he once loved.

"That's a very bold color," he replied.

"Indeed. Bold matches my personality," I chuckled. "But that's not what I wanted to show you. As I learned all the nooks and crannies of this estate, I discovered a secret passageway leading to a grand chamber."

Emery nodded. "There are many hidden passages within the home. I've found many of them myself."

His words were slurring together. Good. That means he's had plenty of wine.

"I doubt you have ever found this passage."

I stopped in front of the familiar wood panel in

the corridor. I ran my hand along the surface until I found the hidden latch. I pressed, and the panel swung open, revealing the secret entrance.

Emery gasped. "No, you're right. I've never found this one before."

He looked up and down the hallway, surveying the other wooden panels. I scanned the hallway as well to make sure we were alone.

"Then let's waste no time and explore. You will not believe where it leads. After you," I gestured for him to enter first.

Emery climbed through the small opening, which was a feat for the rotund man. I followed, snapping the panel back in place, shrouding us in darkness.

"Alex, do you have a light? I can't see a thing," he said.

I clicked on my flashlight, revealing the brick stairs which spiraled downward in front of us.

"Where does it go?"

"You'll see."

I took the lead. Emery's breathing quickened as his heavy feet plodded behind me. For a fat man, he was good at keeping up.

"My God," he exclaimed.

My light illuminated the vaulted room. It was grand and spacious, certainly an impressive space. I often wondered in the long hours spent down here in the dark, preparing for this very moment, what the room's intended use was. There was nothing in it but space. It was as large as the ballroom directly above us and half as grand.

The best part was it was silent - we couldn't hear the loud music or even the dancing feet. What pleased me most was that my guests above wouldn't hear Emery's screams.

Chapter Four

"I had no idea this was even here," Emery said.

He walked over to one of the brick walls and ran his fingers along the mortar.

"This is incredible. I wonder what it was used for."

"I have an idea of what it's for. Come see for yourself."

I beckoned to the far side of the room with my light. Emery strode past me, his curiosity overcoming him. I kept my light directed at the floor, so he couldn't see what awaited him.

The time had come at last. I clenched the flashlight in my hand and rose it high. I brought it down hard on the back of Emery's head, the satisfying crack echoing in the chamber.

He stumbled forward, stunned. I seized his arms

and ran him forward until he collided with the wall within the niche. Another satisfying crack.

I clamped his wrists in iron restraints and chained him to the bricks. His inebriated state made it easy for me to overpower him.

"What- what are you doing?" He slurred.

I spread a line of mortar on the ground in the alcove's opening. On top of it, I placed a layer of bricks. More mortar. More bricks. One row at a time, I built a wall.

"What are you doing?" He asked again, the chains rattling as he struggled in vain.

I ignored him and concentrated on my work. With each row of bricks, I made right the wrongs he did to me. Claiming my ideas as his own. Insulting me whenever he could. Sleeping with my fiancé.

Emery's questions turned to screams, screams that echoed around me. Soon, his upright brick coffin would mute his cries.

I hurried my pace. Before long, the bricks reached the level of his shoulders. I was nearly finished.

I shone my light into the niche to take one last look at my victim. Emery Bernand. I smiled. He still wore his wolf mask from the party. The jester had beaten the wolf. I laughed in my victory.

I finished my work and brushed off my hands,

leaving the flashlight on the floor outside Emery's tomb. I didn't need it to find my way back.

Emery's muffled screams and the sound of rattling chains faded as I crossed the room and entered the passage leading back up to the lively party.

Chapter Five

After freshening up in the washroom, I returned to my guests. They hadn't noticed my absence, which worked well for my alibi. The entertainment I provided distracted everyone. Everyone except Justine.

She spied me the moment I reentered the ballroom. Her hips swayed as she walked toward me, her red dress flowing behind her like a drop of blood suspended in water. Justine's green eyes studied me through her ruby-encrusted fox mask.

"Where's Emery?" she asked.

"He was too drunk to stand, so I called a cab to take him home."

She folded her arms. "I don't believe you."

Justine was too clever for her own good. There were plenty of niches in the cavern below this room -

I could easily wall her up right next to her lover. The very thought of her cheating on me with Emery made my blood boil. If she caused trouble, she would be next.

"Believe what you want. I don't have time to debate this with you. I have guests to attend to."

I brushed past her and helped myself to a glass of wine.

For the next hour, I mingled with the social elite. Everyone had come for me. I talked with peacocks, cats, zebras, lions, and elk. But no wolves. The only wolf here was chained and walled up in the chamber beneath this room.

"It was a wise investment to buy this property for yourself," a man in a deer mask said. "I would have purchased it myself if you hadn't beaten me to it."

He chuckled and raised his glass in a toast. Only, his laugh sounded like scratching, not a laugh at all.

I took my leave of him and went to talk to someone else. They opened their mouth to speak, but instead of words I heard scratching. Horrible scratching, like an animal trying to dig through stone. I cringed at the sound and spun around to speak to someone who would say actual words.

I found a woman in a blue dress wearing a bluebird mask.

"Are you enjoying the party? Do you have enough to drink?" I asked, almost frantically.

The bluebird smiled. The sound of scratching came from her mouth as she did so.

I shuddered. What was going on? Where was this scratching coming from? It drowned out all the other sounds around me. It was everywhere, yet coming from nowhere.

Justine was smirking at me from the corner. She must know something.

I rushed over to her and clasped my hands on her bare shoulders.

"Where is that scratching coming from? Do you hear it?" I demanded of her.

She pursed her lips at me. "Now it seems you've had too much to drink. I only hear boring conversations and loud music."

She was no use. The scratching grew louder. I had to know if anyone else could hear it. I approached a man with his back to me. I tapped his shoulder.

"Do you hear that scratching?"

He turned to face me. Gasping, I dropped my drink. The glass shattered on the floor. I stumbled back at the sight of the man in a wolf mask. Emery.

"I don't hear anything," he said.

His voice was deep, not Emery's high pitch shrill. I apologized for my faux pas and left the man.

The scratching grew more frantic. It was faster and louder than ever. It was desperate, just like me. I had to find out where it was coming from.

I returned to the woman in the blue dress. She might know something. I tapped her shoulder from behind. She turned around, and I fell to the floor. She wasn't a bluebird anymore; she was a wolf.

I scooted away from her. Everyone was facing me now. They formed a circle around me, viewing the man in the jester mask trembling on the floor. They were all wolves.

Chapter Six

I screamed. The scratching continued. Scratching, scratching, scratching. It was too much. It was everywhere. The wolves were closing in on me. They knew what I had done. They knew of my plan to kill Emery.

"It's not too late," I said to them, defiantly. "I can tear down the wall."

The only response was more scratching.

Justine in her fox mask and a wolf stepped through the crowd. The wolf laughed and lifted his mask.

In my shock, I only got two words out.

"Emery. How?"

Justine must have found him, she must have freed him.

"How am I here? I think the real question is, how are you here?"

He was speaking in riddles. Nothing made sense.

I covered my ears. I couldn't think over the incessant scratching. It was deafening.

"I left you down there. I trapped you. There's no way you could have escaped."

"But was it me?" Emery knelt in front of me. "You hear the scratching, no one else can. Why would that be? Why is it that only you can hear it?"

"Because," I shook my head. "Because you were never the one inside the wall."

Emery stood and returned to Justine, wrapping his arm around her waist.

She laughed at me, an evil cackle of a laugh. Emery laughed. Everyone gathered around laughed at me. I covered my face with my hands, trying to shield myself from their torment.

When I removed my hands, it was quiet. The scratching ceased. The laughing ceased. I looked around the room. Everyone was as they were before. They all donned their original masks, not a wolf to be seen. They were dancing, eating, and drinking.

They were oblivious to the trembling jester on the floor. The room grew dim and everything around me faded. The dancing figures turned into nothing more than shadows. My entire world grew dark, save for one sliver of light at the center of my vision.

My other senses returned to me. A musty scent overwhelmed my nostrils and burned my eyes. My fingers throbbed with pain. Why did my fingers hurt?

The slit in the bricks cast just enough light to see by. I peered down at my hands. They were wet with blood. My fingernails were gone. The fleshy tips of my fingers were worn down to the bone.

I screamed in agony. The scratching - it had been me.

I was the one scratching at the brick wall.

I was immured in this hidden alcove.

I was chained to the wall.

I was lured into the secret chamber beneath the ballroom.

I was the one who lost my fortune and forced to sell my family's estate.

I was the one who had an affair with Justine.

I was the one who wronged Emery.

It was me all along. Alex, not Emery.

Emery had brought his vengeance down upon me. Would I die of starvation? Or maybe suffocation? No. The narrow gap between two bricks, which allowed the light to seep in, also allowed air in. I would have plenty of oxygen, but no food, no water.

I couldn't perish like this. I had to get out. The chains rattled as I raised my hands.

I clawed at the wall. My protruding finger bones scraped frantically down the wall, each stroke against the bricks causing searing pain. But I persisted. I had to get out.

"Help me! Let me out!"

Over and over I yelled. Over and over I scratched.

I scratched until the little sliver of light went dark.

I scratched until I had no strength left.

I scratched until my head slumped forward, the little bells of my jester mask jingling with the movement. I closed my eyes, too weak to scratch anymore.

Acknowledgments

A special thanks to Laura E. Perez for putting together the Thrill of the Hunt anthologies. This short story was originally featured in the Thrill of the Hunt: Buried Alive anthology. When writing this tale, I took inspiration from one of my all-time favorite authors: Edgar Allan Poe.

I would like to thank Juli's Elite Editing for making sure my writing is on point and my story comes to life. Thank you to Rene with Phycel Designs for creating this gorgeous cover. When she showed it to me, it blew my mind. She did an amazing job of capturing the essence of this story visually.

A special thank you to my family, friends, and readers. You inspire me to keep writing so I can share my stories with the world. I hope you reading enjoyed this story!

About the Author

Valerie Puri is an author of Paranormal, Fantasy, and Young Adult.

As an author of both short stories and novels, she enjoys the flexibility of writing tales of any length. Her favorite aspect of writing is the ability to create something out of nothing. She loves building worlds readers can visualize and filling those worlds with complex characters and storylines. Valerie believes that the experiences we have in life are just stories waiting to be written.

In 2016, she published her debut novel, The Crimson Tree, a thrilling paranormal tale inspired by true events. The main source of inspiration for this story was a number of experiences her sister encountered in her home. She went on to publish The Dociles, book one of The Secret Archives Trilogy, her young adult dystopian series. Valerie's work can be found in anthologies such as Demonic Anthologies, Thrill of the Hunt, and We Know the Truth, Do You? Readers can look forward to future novels and short stories with paranormal and urban fantasy aspects in the near future.

When she's not writing, she enjoys spending time with her family, traveling, or listening to audio books. She is a Florida transplant, but part of her will always call the Midwest home.

<u>www.valeriepuri.com</u>